Moi & Marie Antoinette

D0473512

by

Lynn Cullen

illustrated by

Amy Young

BLOOMSBURY

LONDON NEW DELHI NEW YORK SYDNEY

Ỿou would think life would be perfect for two adorable creatures such as Antoinette and myself. And indeed it was . . . until that fateful morning. I was besting Antoinette at tug of war with some freshly stolen bloomers, when we were called to the Empress's chamber. I barked in protest as we rushed down the palace halls.

"Hush, Sébastien," said Antoinette. "We shall play later."

Before I could utter another yap, I found myself in the glittering presence of Her Royal Highness, the Empress of Austria, Antoinette's mama.

The Empress looked up from her papers.
"You look small for thirteen, daughter.
Have you been eating your fish?"
Antoinette held me close.
Like me, she hated the taste of
anything that had once swum.
"Yes, Mama."

"Do you allow yourself to be properly washed
and combed each day?"
Antoinette hugged me closer. Like me, she was
naturally stunning and felt little need to be
groomed.
"Yes, Mama."

"Are you afraid of thunder, or the dark, or
any such foolish thing?"

Antoinette squeezed me tight. We both knew
that neither thunder nor the dark were the least
bit foolish. We were scared to pieces of them.

"No, Mama."

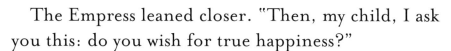

The Empress leaned closer. "Then, my child, I ask
you this: do you wish for true happiness?"

If the Empress was offering soft pillows
or tender morsels of chicken, of course
we wanted them. I licked Antoinette's
face in encouragement.

"Yes, Mama," said Antoinette. "I do."

"Good," said the Empress. "A rare
chance for happiness has come your way.
The King of France wishes you to marry
his grandson, who shall be king himself
someday. I have said yes. You shall leave
as soon as you are presentable."

This news was not as exciting as tender
morsels of chicken, but I would have to
make do.

It takes time to get ready to marry a future king. As I grew from a darling pup into a handsome dog, Antoinette was told to stop skipping and taught to glide like a queen. She had to have her teeth straightened and her hair curled. She had to stop playing with dolls and start playing the harp.

I myself was already perfect.

At last, my Antoinette was stuffed into a new gown, strung with jewels and packed into a fine carriage. Off to France she went, accompanied by one hundred ladies, two hundred servants, three hundred horses . . . and Moi.

For weeks, we trundled down muddy roads lined with cheering townspeople. I thought my tail would uncurl from boredom. At last, we reached a river with an island in the middle of it.

"Look, Sébastien!" said Antoinette. "On the other side of the river is France!"

We were rowed to the only house on the island. There, Antoinette was ordered to leave everything from her old life behind. Before I could locate a single snack, Antoinette was stripped of her horses, her servants, her ladies, her dress! Naked as a newborn pup, she stepped into clothes befitting a French queen.

"Antoinette!" I barked as they led her away. "Don't forget me!"

She put up such a fuss, she'd hardly made it into France before she was slipped the only reminder of her past . . .

Moi.

The new palace was so large, I could see it would take me days to claim it properly for myself.

"Oh, Sébastien!" said Antoinette. "France is far grander than I imagined. Mama was right — I shall be so very happy here."

Until I tasted the chicken, I would reserve my judgement.

Antoinette's wedding was the next day, during a thunderstorm. Thousands of people in sodden fancy attire pressed closer to get a glimpse of my Antoinette.

Few knew that under her diamond-covered skirt there quaked a certain fine creature . . . Moi.

We made our way to the chapel, where we met a large boy hardly older than Antoinette. I was prepared to nip his lace-covered ankles – until I noticed his face. He was more terrified than Moi. Shaking like a royal rattle, he placed a ring on Antoinette's finger. A cheer went up all over France.

But being married to the future king was not all juicy snacks and squishy pillows.

From morning until night, bothersome crowds surrounded my poor Antoinette. A swarm of tiresome ladies woke her each day, dressed her as if she were a doll, then ushered her to church.

Afterwards, they sat her at dinner, where any Frenchman
in the kingdom could watch her every bite.

Moi? I was left to gnaw on chair legs and water the statues.

It was a rare day when I saw her alone. On one such afternoon, I made great sport on the palace lawn with the King's best wig, but she paid little attention.

"You know, Sébastien," she said, "perhaps when I am Queen and not merely a princess, I shall be happier."

I hustled to retrieve the acorn she had thrown. Did she think *I* was rolling over with joy these days?

"Play with Moi!" I barked. "Play with Moi! Moi! Moi!"

Antoinette rose and then, as if I was not there, walked slowly back to the palace. I buried the acorn in a fit of fury.

Then one day, the old King died. Antoinette and the frightened boy in the lace socks became Queen and King.

"Now that I am Queen," Antoinette announced, "I may do things my own way. Then I shall finally be happy."

I perked up, expecting her immediate call, but to my shock, a dressmaker was fetched instead.

She soon had my Antoinette decked out in more layers than a royal wedding cake. But that did not make Antoinette happier. Then Antoinette tried smothering herself in jewels, and when that did not suit, she teased and tugged and tortured her hair into a towering pouf.

Her hair was so high that whenever she dashed off to one of her
dazzling parties, she had to kneel on the floor of the carriage.

Time passed — enough for a thousand glittering nights to swirl by while my chin turned grey. Just when I thought it could be no worse, Antoinette gave birth to a *baby*. Why would she do such a thing? She had Moi!

I retreated to the park, as forgotten as yesterday's bone.

Six long years passed. Six! Until one morning in the park, I was awakened by a child. I blinked. It was young Antoinette! She had come back to me! My head cleared. It was not Antoinette, but her daughter. My gorgeous fur bristled along my back.

"Mama had another baby today. A boy," she sighed. "Now she will never have time for me."

Humpf, I sniffed. The child thought she had troubles. What about *Moi*?

Just then, a clap of thunder shook the park. Before I could run to the palace for shelter, the child latched onto my lovely self. "I'm scared of thunder," she whispered.

A shout came from the palace before I could shake her off. "Madame Thérèse!" called a nurse. "It is time for your supper! We have some delicious fish."

The child shuddered, then buried her face in my fur. "I hate fish!"

I craned my neck around to get a better view. Who was this child?

I don't know why, but I gave her an acorn. Her mother would have known just what to do with it, but would this child?

Good heavens, the child could throw!

I followed her into the palace, where she found a ball. I thought our fun would have no end!

Just then the child was called to the Queen's chamber.

Before I could protest, the child scooped me up and took me along.

Antoinette looked up from her cards. She seemed surprised to see me. Was that a smile I spied before she turned to her daughter?

"Thérèse," she said, "for a child of six, you look small. Have you been eating your fish?"

Thérèse held me close. I knew that, like me, she hated anything that had once swum.

"Yes, Mama."

"Do you allow yourself to be properly washed and combed each day?"

Thérèse hugged me closer. Like me, she was naturally stunning and had little need for grooming.

"Yes, Mama."

"Are you afraid of thunder, or the dark, or any such foolish thing?"

Even if Thérèse had not been squeezing me tight, I could have scarcely breathed. I had heard these words before.

"No, Mama," said Thérèse.

Antoinette put down her cards.

"Do you wish for true happiness, child?"

The child had me in her grip. If only I could squirm loose and warn her, "No, no, **a thousand times no!**"

Thérèse thumped me between the ears.

"But, Mama," she said, "I have Sébastien. I *am* **happy.**"

And Antoinette, gazing at me, smiled.

Not a thousand sweet treats nor a million soft pillows could bring the joy that spilled from my grateful heart. Over and over I licked Thérèse's dear cheek — and then I stopped.

I gave Antoinette my paw. As we three gathered close, I knew someone who had found at last the truest of happiness:

Moi

~Author's Note~

THE ARCHDUCHESS MARIE ANTONIA JOSEPHINA JOHANNA (called Antonia or Antoinette by her family) was born on November 2 1755, the fifteenth child of Maria Theresa, Empress of Austria. Like all rulers of her time, Antoinette's mother used her children to make marriages that would strengthen her empire. The Empress saved the most important marriage for her youngest daughter, Antoinette.

In order to marry the future King of France, Antoinette had to give up all her Austrian ways, including speaking her native language. She left home for the palace at Versailles near Paris when she was fourteen — never to return. She was allowed to take only a few personal possessions. One was a little pug dog, whom I've chosen to call Sébastien.

Antoinette's wedding was on May 16 1770. The marriage wasn't a happy one. When spectacular hairstyles, clothes and jewellery brought no peace, Antoinette had an entire make-believe village built where she could live in elegant simplicity and dote on her young children.

In 1789, thousands of families went starving because of a crop failure and the government would not help them. The people looked for someone to blame and Antoinette was the most obvious target — though her expenses were not the main reason France was suffering a financial crisis. In truth, a fortune had been spent supporting the American colonies during the Revolutionary War.

The hungry people of Paris did not know or care about this. On October 6 1789, a crowd of fifteen thousand furious women stormed Versailles and seized Antoinette and her family. Three years later, Antoinette was put to death.

Marie Antoinette's daughter, Thérèse, survived and, following her mother's dying wish, married her cousin to become the Duchess d'Angoulême.

Today Versailles offers visitors a look into the glittering world of the eighteenth-century French court. I like to imagine that one of the many old trees growing in the park was planted in play by Marie Antoinette's beloved pug.

To Audrey and Thomas
with grateful acknowledgement to Ann Cooper and Nelly Rey
— A. Y.

For Megan
— L. C.

Bloomsbury Publishing, London, New Delhi, New York and Sydney

First published in Great Britain in 2006 by Bloomsbury Publishing Plc
50 Bedford Square, London, WC1B 3DP

This paperback edition first published in August 2008

First published in America in 2006 by Bloomsbury USA Children's Books
175 Fifth Avenue, New York, NY 10010

Text copyright © Lynn Cullen 2006
Illustrations copyright © Amy Young 2006
The moral rights of the author and illustrator have been asserted

All rights reserved
No part of this publication may be reproduced or transmitted by any means, electronic, mechanical,
photocopying or otherwise, without the prior permission of the publisher

A CIP catalogue record for this book is available from the British Library

ISBN 978 0 7475 9774 2

The illustrations in this book were created using gouache
on Fabriano Uno soft press watercolour paper

Typeset in MrsEaves
Designed by Teresa K. Dikun
Printed in China by South China Printing Company, Dongguan City, Guangdong

3 5 7 9 8 6 4

All papers used by Bloomsbury Publishing are natural, recyclable products made from wood grown in well-managed
forests. The manufacturing processes conform to the environmental regulations of the country of origin.

www.bloomsbury.com